CUTLASS
IN THE SNOW

". . . a lot to tell about . . ."

ELIZABETH SHUB

CUTLASS
IN THE
SNOW

PICTURES BY RACHEL ISADORA

GREENWILLOW BOOKS, NEW YORK

Library of Congress Cataloging in Publication Data
Shub, Elizabeth.   Cutlass in the snow.
Summary: In 1797 Sam and his grandfather explore the
wild and uninhabited Fire Island, just missing a band
of pirates but finding a cutlass and buried treasure.
1. Children's stories, American. [1. Fire Island (N.Y.)—Fiction.
2. Pirates—Fiction. 3. Buried treasure—Fiction.
4. Grandfathers—Fiction]   I. Isadora, Rachel, ill.   II. Title.
PZ7.S5592Cu 1986   [Fic]   85-5442
ISBN 0-688-05927-9   ISBN 0-688-05928-7 (lib bdg.)

FOR J.B.

CONTENTS

CUTLASS
IN THE SNOW

There are events so strange or unlikely that in time people stop believing that they really happened. Over the years they are told by parents to children, by neighbors to friends, until the truth is slowly forgotten. They become stories, local legends. But sometimes, long after the events took place, something is found, an old letter, a document, a ledger, and the truth is rediscovered. This is such a story.

"The sail filled, the boat steadied, and they were off . . ."

CHAPTER 1

The Weather Better Hold

In 1797, all of New York's Long Island was farm country. The farms of Sam's parents and his grandfather were next door to each other. Grandpa Campbell was a widower, and Sam often stayed with him overnight.

One evening late in November, Grandpa and Sam were having their supper, and talking about Fire Island. Only a short distance across Great South Bay, the island was a wild, uninhabited place. Like other Long Islanders, Grandpa went there to hunt raccoon. There were stories that thieves and pirates came to the island, but Grandpa said he'd never seen anyone there except for a fellow hunter.

"Sam," Grandpa said, "I have an idea. Since tomorrow is Saturday, how would you like to see the island for yourself? We can sail there in the morning, if the weather holds, that is."

"It better hold," Sam said.

"No hunting this time," Grandpa said. "There's too much just for you to see. We'll picnic and bring back some holly. It's only a few weeks to Christmas."

It was still dark, as Grandpa and Sam walked down to the beach the next morning. The weather was clear and not too cold. The wind was fair, the tide had just turned ebb, the right direction for the trip.

16

Grandpa's boat lay on a mooring. His skiff was beached on the sand, well above the high-water line. Sam helped Grandpa roll it on logs down to the water's edge. Sam had learned how to pick up the back log quickly as the skiff was about to roll off it, and place the log at the forward end.

The sun was coming up as they reached the boat. Grandpa made fast the skiff and Sam got into the boat. Grandpa passed Sam the day's provisions: meat, cheese, two loaves of bread, two bottles of water, a bottle of cider, a teapot, and a tin of tea.

At last Grandpa climbed into the boat. After the sail had been set, he told Sam to cast off the mooring line. Grandpa tamed the flapping sail and put the tiller hard over. The sail filled, the boat steadied, and they were off, the skiff towing smoothly behind them.

*"The wind is so strong here that it prunes the trees
like a gardener . . ."*

CHAPTER 2

The Surprise

It was about a two-hour trip across Great South Bay. Grandpa figured they would sail home in the late afternoon, riding the flood current to the east.

The sky was as blue as only an autumn sky can be. Out in the bay, the wind was just strong enough to raise small ripples. Sam watched as the bow of the boat sliced neatly through them.

As the sun rose higher, the day got warmer,

but it was still quite cold on deck. Grandpa sent Sam below to warm up. He was back again in minutes. Grandpa smiled.

"That was quick," he said.

Grandpa took in the sail a bit as they rounded Blue Point and headed for Point o' Woods. It seemed to Sam that no time at all had passed when Grandpa said, "We'll be coming to anchor in about twenty minutes."

And about twenty minutes later, Grandpa brought the boat into the wind some thirty yards from a beach. Sam let the anchor down as the boat came to a stop. He secured the anchor and hurried back to help furl the sail. They hauled in the skiff, got into it, and rowed ashore.

Grandpa, with Sam's help, pulled the skiff up on the beach and anchored it.

It was the loneliest place Sam had ever been. The only sound was the lapping of the waves. A few gulls flew overhead and tiny sandpipers hurried back and forth along the beach.

A tall dune stretched along the shoreline. Grandpa pointed to a low, flat gap in it, beyond which Sam could see an outcropping of trees.

"We could go straight through the break," Grandpa said, "but we're going to climb to the top of the dune first. There's something I want you to see. It's a surprise."

From the top of the dune, as far as Sam could see, he looked down on what seemed to be a never-ending flat green roof.

"The wind is so strong here that it prunes the trees, like a gardener," Grandpa said. "Cuts the tops right off them. That's why they're so even.

"See that ridge behind the trees," Grandpa added. "That's the top of another dune, even taller than this one, and beyond it is the ocean beach, and the ocean."

"A deer came to the clearing . . ."

CHAPTER 3

In the Forest

They climbed down and made their way into the forest. The ancient floor was a soft carpet of leaf mold and humus. The foliage was so thick that no sound of the ocean came through. Only the calls of startled birds broke the silence.

"Look, Grandpa, there's a holly tree," Sam cried.

"Yes," Grandpa said, "you'll see them all over the forest. Let's find a place to make camp first, and have something to eat. We've got a lot to do."

Soon they came to a clearing. Grandpa said it was a good spot. He quickly made a small fire with twigs Sam helped him gather. Grandpa boiled some water to make tea. They sat down to rest and eat.

A deer came to the clearing, stopped, looked at Sam and Grandpa, and quickly disappeared.

"Did you notice how large his antlers were?" Grandpa said. "That was an old buck." A rabbit hopped into view, and darted away again. Two raccoons looked down from their trees, chattered a bit, and quickly climbed out of sight. They made Sam laugh.

"All right, Sam," Grandpa said, when they had

finished eating, "let's put this fire out." Grandpa stamped it out and they kicked dirt over the ashes.

"We'll walk over to the ocean now, and you can have your first look at the great Atlantic."

*"The gray-green ocean lay in an immense
half-circle before them."*

CHAPTER 4

The Ocean Beach

They left the clearing and picked up a rough path to the ocean beach. White sand stretched for miles in each direction. The gray-green ocean lay in an immense half-circle before them.

Sam looked at Grandpa. "It's different from the bay," he said.

"You can't see the other shore, and the water seems endless," Grandpa said. "On the bay, wherever you are, you can see both shores. The bay looks more like a river."

The ocean was calm and smooth, but small, foamy waves broke against the shore and fell back, leaving hard, wet sand behind. For a moment Sam watched the bubbles forming in the backwash. Then as a wave receded, he ran forward, and just made it back to dry sand as the next wave rushed in.

They walked and walked. Sam raced the waves. He searched the beach for shells, and found so many he wanted, his pockets were stuffed and finally so were Grandpa's.

"Time to pick holly," Grandpa said, and they went back to the forest. By late afternoon, Sam had gathered enough holly to decorate his parents' farmhouse, Grandpa's farmhouse, and there was some to spare to give to neighbors.

Heavily laden, they trudged slowly back to the

skiff. As they rowed out to the boat, Grandpa glanced up at the sky. "Well," he said, "it looks as if the weather is changing." The sky was darkening with clouds and the wind had shifted to the east. By the time they reached the boat, it had begun to snow.

"I think we had better spend the night right here on the boat and wait out the weather," Grandpa said. "They'll understand and won't worry at home when they see the snow. We've got plenty of blankets and some food left, and I'd rather sail in the daylight."

After they had eaten, Sam, wrapped in blankets, went to sleep on the boards which made up the bench bunk in the little cabin. The boat rocked slightly as it tugged at its anchor. The snow fell silently on the deck. After a while Grandpa stretched out on a bench bed on the other side of the boat and he, too, fell asleep.

*"Suddenly he saw a light on the land, and then
another and another . . ."*

CHAPTER 5

Lights in the Night

Sam woke in the middle of the night. It seemed warmer. He decided to see whether it was still snowing. He pushed his blankets back, and quietly, so as not to disturb Grandpa, groped his way over the bunk to the hatch. Carefully he pushed forward the hatch cover and looked out. The snow had stopped, leaving about an inch of white on the cockpit floor

31

and bench. Sam looked up into a clear, star-filled sky. An almost full moon sat in the west. Sam could see where they had beached the skiff that afternoon.

Suddenly he saw a light on the land, and then another and another. They were moving. Sam quickly crawled back into the cabin.

"Grandpa, Grandpa," he whispered, shaking him by the shoulder.

Grandpa was awake at once.

"There are lights out there," Sam said.

"Out where?" Grandpa asked.

"On the shore, in the woods, I think," Sam replied.

Grandpa made his way to the hatch. The lights were still there.

"Whoever they are, they must have come in from the ocean side, or they would have seen us,"

Grandpa said in a quiet voice. "The most sensible thing to do, I guess, is to stay up and see what happens. Get the blankets, Sam, we'll go up on deck and keep watch."

Sam got the blankets and, covered from head to foot, they settled down to wait.

"Are they pirates?" Sam asked.

"I hope we'll never find out," Grandpa said.

Excitement kept Sam awake. Just before the dawn the lights began to move again.

"They're moving away from us," Grandpa said. In a moment he added, "They're moving toward the ocean side." The lights became dimmer, blacked out from time to time and then were gone.

"Sam ran around inspecting them and almost tripped over something sticking up out of the snow . . ."

CHAPTER 6

The Cutlass

Soon the eastern sky was alight with sunrise.
"Grandpa, can't we go back to the island for a little, before we sail home?"

"Well, Sam, I don't think we'll solve the mystery of the lights, if that's what you have in mind,
but we can have a look before we start back. The
wind is northwest, fine to sail home on, and the
tide will turn in our favor a little after noon."

35

They rowed back to the island. There was a light covering of snow on the ground.

"Let's go to the clearing," Sam said.

"Good idea," said Grandpa.

Sam walked behind Grandpa, so that he could place his feet in the footprints Grandpa made.

"Over the dune or through the gap?" Grandpa asked.

"Up and over," Sam said, "to see the flat trees again."

From the top of the dune, the treetops looked as if they had been sprinkled with sugar. Sam made a snowball, threw it, and slid down the dune after it. Grandpa climbed carefully down to him.

Sam was still trying to walk in Grandpa's footprints, when suddenly he stopped and tugged at Grandpa's sleeve.

"Look, Grandpa! There are other footprints!"

The footprints led into the clearing. There were at least four or five different sets, zigzagging over it. Sam ran around inspecting them, and almost tripped over something sticking up out of the snow. It was a cutlass. Grandpa picked it up, examined it, and looked thoughtfully down at the footprints. "I'll wager these'll take us right to the ocean path," he said. He motioned Sam to follow him. The prints ran right along the rough path Grandpa and Sam had taken the day before, all the way to the water's edge. In the snowy sand there were marks of a large ship's boat. The ocean looked gray and choppy. There was no sign of a ship.

"Whoever they were, they're gone," Grandpa said.

"Pirates!" Sam cried. "I'm sure they were pirates."

"Maybe so," Grandpa said.

"It's a find, all right," Grandpa said. "It's a find."

CHAPTER 7

The Chest

They made their way back to the clearing.
Grandpa looked carefully at the spot
where the cutlass had been. He bent
down, probing with the cutlass. The ground was
soft, beneath the snow, as if someone had been
digging there. The blade quickly cut through dry
leaves and humus. Only a few inches down, it
struck something.

"I've hit something, Sam," Grandpa cried. "I'll dig and. you push the dirt away with your hands."

It wasn't long before they unearthed a chest. It was not large, but it was heavy.

"I told you it was pirates," Sam said, "and the cutlass marked the spot."

"Pirates or no, they sure were in a hurry," Grandpa said. "Probably left the cutlass behind by accident, maybe a lucky one for us."

"Do you think there is a treasure in the chest?" Sam asked.

"We'll soon see," Grandpa said, "when we get it back to the boat."

Grandpa had to rest often before they got the chest to the skiff, and once on the boat, he had a hard time prying the chest open. As the lid finally came up, they saw only crumpled paper. But

40

when Grandpa lifted away the paper, they saw that the chest was filled with gold coins.

"I told you!" Sam cried, jumping up and down. "I told you!"

"It's a find, all right," Grandpa said. "It's a find."

Grandpa picked up one of the gold coins. He closed the box, smiled, and handed the coin to Sam. "Here's a keepsake for you, Sam," he said.

". . . but in the ledger dated 1798, there were some surprising entries."

CHAPTER 8

The Ledgers

Sam had a lot to tell about when he got home. The whole community talked of nothing but the treasure Grandpa and Sam had found. For a time Grandpa thought that someone might come forth to claim it, but no one did. In the end the source of the treasure and who had buried it remained a mystery.

Grandpa told the story for years and years but as time went on, people believed it less and less. By the time Sam was grown, only Sam and Grandpa remembered it was true.

Grandpa was over ninety when he died. He left his farm and all his money to Sam. Among the careful records Grandpa had kept, Sam found his book of accounts for the year 1798. On impulse, Sam got some paper and glue, and pasted a makeshift envelope on the inside back cover. He carefully wrapped the gold coin Grandpa had given him in a bit of cloth, placed it in the envelope, closed the ledger, and put it back on the shelf with all the others.

Sam, too, lived long and in turn left the property to his son Sam, and so it went down the generations until more than a hundred years had passed.

It was 1907, and what had been farmland was now a town, but the old farmhouse still stood. It, too, was changed and modernized, and a Sam Campbell lived there, with his wife Louisa, two daughters, Susan and Mary, and ten-year-old Sam, the sixth Sam.

One day when father and son were cleaning out the attic, young Sam became curious about an old trunk that stood in a corner. When they opened it, they were surprised to find, beneath some worn clothes, several yellowed books of account. They bore the name Sam Campbell and contained meticulous records over a period of years.

Sums for the sale of cattle, horses, timber, as well as small items, were carefully recorded. Each entry was dated and described in detail. The accounts varied little over the years, but in a ledger dated 1798 there were some surprising entries. There were several listings of unusually large sums of money. And what was equally strange, unlike all the other listings, there was no exact date, and no description of any transactions to show where the money had come from.

It was young Sam who noticed the makeshift envelope at the back of the ledger. And when they unwrapped the gold coin, his father gave it to Sam to keep as his own.

The news of the ledger's discovery and the finding of the gold coin was talked about by all the relatives, and it wasn't long before an elderly cousin recalled the old family story of the Fire Island treasure Grandpa and Sam had found.

Grandpa's story, and how the long lost truth came to light, is still told in the Campbell family. Descendants of Grandpa still live in the old farmhouse, and the gold coin, generation after generation, is given to the eldest Campbell boy on his tenth birthday.

ELIZABETH SHUB is the author of *Seeing Is Believing* and *The White Stallion,* both ALA Notable Books. She is noted for her translations of folk and fairy tales and in 1982 was selected for the IBBY (International Board on Books for Young Children) Honor List for translation. Mrs. Shub's translations include *About Wise Men and Simpletons,* a collection of twelve tales from the Brothers Grimm, an ALA Notable. With the author, she has also translated many of the children's stories of Isaac Bashevis Singer.

RACHEL ISADORA, once a professional ballerina, now devotes her full time to writing, illustrating, and painting. She is the author-artist of many successful picture books including *Ben's Trumpet,* a Caldecott Honor Book and a Boston Globe-Horn Book Honor Book, *Opening Night, I Hear, I See,* and *I Touch.* She is the illustrator of *Seeing Is Believing* and *The White Stallion,* both by Elizabeth Shub.